The Cay

I0614944

Grades 7-8

Written by Fran Van Vorst
Illustrated by Ric Ward

ISBN 1-55035-622-4
Copyright 1998
Revised January 2006
All Rights Reserved * Printed in Canada

Published in the United States by:
On the Mark Press
3909 Witmer Road PMB 175
Niagara Falls, New York
14305
www.onthemarkpress.com

Published in Canada by:
S&S Learning Materials
15 Dairy Avenue
Napanee, Ontario
K7R 1M4
www.sslearning.com

© On the Mark Press • S&S Learning Materials   1   OTM-14212 • SSN1-212 The Cay

Look For Other Intermediate - Novel Studies

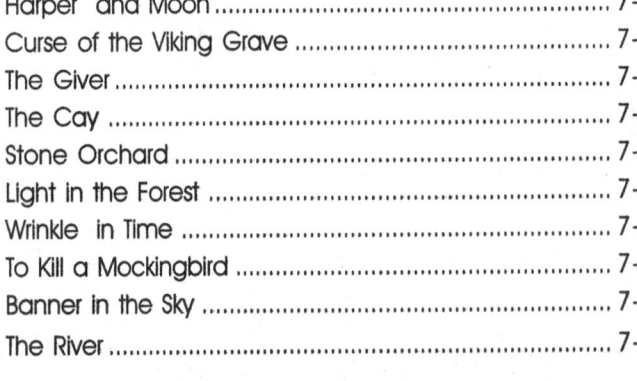

Table of Contents

THE CAY
BY THEODORE TAYLOR

Expectations

The students will:

- develop and reinforce many reading skills.

- become aware of how people can overcome a disability and fight to survive.

- understand how a person's attitude and feelings can change.

Summary of the Story

The Cay

The Cay is an adventure story filled with excitement as well as a struggle for survival. Phillip, an American lad, lived with his parents on the Dutch island of Curacao, which is off the coast of Venezuela. The story took place during World War II when German submarines were poised to strike at important industrial landmarks or ships and tankers that plied the waters of the South Atlantic. Phillip's mother, who disliked living on such a remote, unpleasant island with people of other races, was determined to return to the U.S. even more expediently when the German bombs and submarines loomed so dangerously close.

Phillip and his mother left for Florida by ship. The ship was torpedoed and sunk. Phillip became separated from his mother and he found that he was afloat on a raft with a black man, Timothy. Phillip, like his mother, disliked black people but this would soon change. An injury to his head left Phillip with a raging headache and eventually blindness. Phillip was even more dependent on Timothy for survival. When they finally beached their raft on a tiny desolate cay, Phillip was about to experience a change in his attitude, his only friend in an alien land.

The hurricane which swept the cay took Timothy's life leaving Phillip alone and in despair. Would he ever be rescued? Would he view black people from now on as valuable, important people?

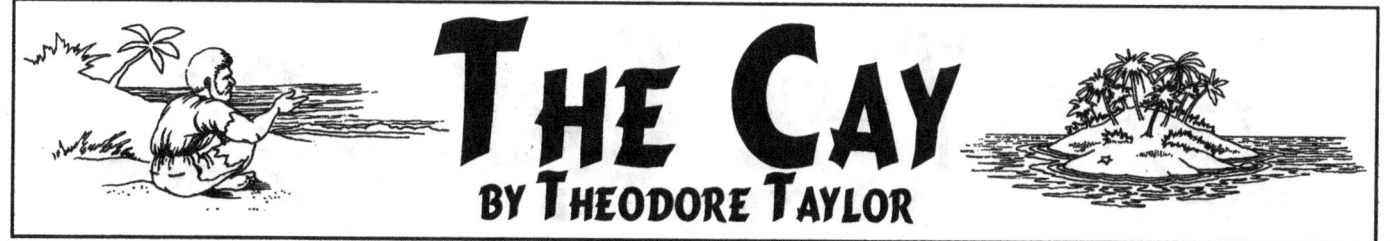

Biography of the Author

Theodore Taylor

Theodore Taylor was born on June 23, 1921 in Stateville, North Carolina. Although his parents were poor, he lived a rich childhood in the beauty of the outdoors. Books became an integral part of his life. He began his writing career at age thirteen working for the Portsmouth, Virginia Star, reporting about high school events. He was a copyboy for the Washington Daily News and had numerous other reporting experiences.

After the Korean War he finally secured production work in Hollywood. His first books, The Magnificent Mitscher, a biography and Fire on the Beaches, were adult books published in 1957. His first book for young readers was People Who Make Movies, largely as a result of his movie work.

By far the best known of Theodore Taylor's children books is The Cay. It takes place during the second world war with the setting being the West Indies and Florida Keys. It is a somewhat controversial story of a prejudiced white boy saved from drowning by a black West Indian sailor. It has been acclaimed to have improved racial understandings and received awards and citations. It received the silver medal of the Commonwealth Club of California in 1969, the Jane Adams Children's Book Award in 1970 and the American Library Association Notable Book Award. It was on all the major critics lists of best books and was made into a film for television. Some groups have criticized the book as being "racist".

Selected Works by Theodore Taylor are:

The Cay

People Who Make Movies

Air Raid - Pearl Harbor!

The Children's War

Timothy of the Cay

The Maldonado Miracle

The Trouble With Tuck

Tuck Triumphant

THE CAY
BY THEODORE TAYLOR

Teacher Input Suggestions

Before You Begin the Book:

Before beginning the literature unit on <u>The Cay</u> with your students, perhaps the following suggestions would be helpful to motivate the children and to develop understanding of different races of people and the attitudes (prejudices) that have developed.

1. Discussion about the title of the <u>The Cay</u>.

2. Predict what the story could be about after reading the title and seeing the cover.

3. Place key words on a chart or blackboard and ask for thoughts or impressions of what the story is about:

   <u>Example</u>:   a young lad   a black man   a small island   raft
                     shipwrecked   hut   hurricane   cat

4. Ask the children to predict whether they think that this story is fiction or nonfiction.

5. Discussion topics:

   a) Has anyone experienced an unusual problem?
   b) Has anyone experienced a frightening situation?
   c) Has anyone been on a large ship?

6. Discussion topics:

   a) What do we mean by the word "a friend"?
   b) What is meant by "prejudice"?

7. List on a chart the types of prejudice that we are aware of that exists.

8. Create a web about "Survival". Make the web on a chart or on the chalkboard.
   Example:

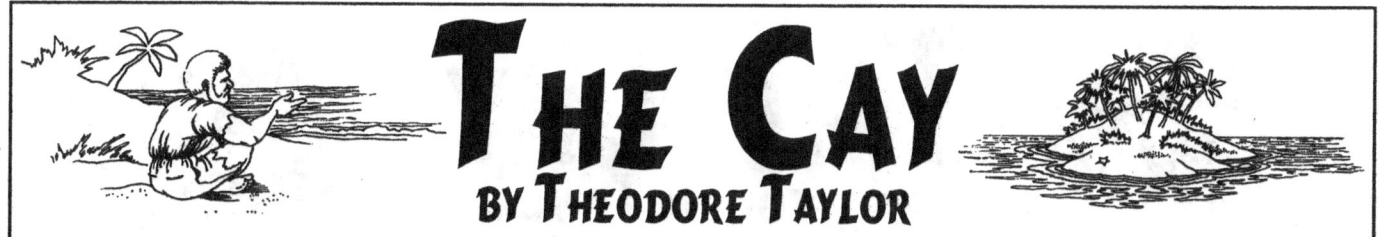
9. Working in small groups, the children should brainstorm ideas and share with the class from their discussion.

    Topic: The students are told that they should imagine they find themselves marooned on a deserted island with one other person.

10. Display the vocabulary words for the first three chapters from page six. Discuss the words and their meanings.

11. Discuss with the students what is meant by the "Character Attribute Webs".

While You Read the Book:

1. The teacher should read the first two chapters with the class and discuss the story questions. There are many vocabulary words, geographical and historical wartime terms that require an explanation for a young reader. The children could buddy read with their classmates for extra practice.

2. The booklet section, although detailed, is provided to present a number of critical thinking skills on Bloom's Levels of Learning.

3. The vocabulary lists are included to be used before the chapter sections. The words could be printed on chart paper. The vocabulary building activities are designed to reinforce the vocabulary and provide enjoyment at the same time.

4. The booklet questions should be discussed carefully before the children work independently.

5. The cooperative and independent activities should be monitored carefully to ensure a good use of time and appropriate participation by each individual.

After Completion of the Book:

The activities provide an extension to the theme of the story and tie it to other parts of the curriculum. It gives the teacher a chance to assess the degree of learning and provides for places where improvement can be made.

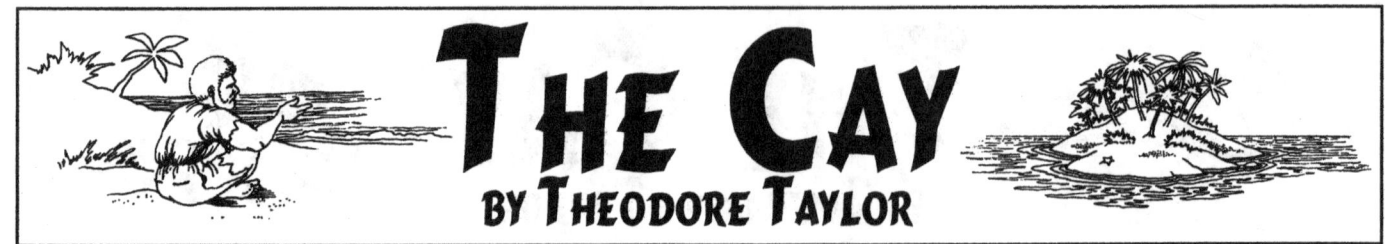

Vocabulary Lists

In this section, the vocabulary words are grouped according to the chapter sections in the booklet.

Chapter 1 (Pages 9 to 17):

refinery (9), diesel (19), pontoon bridge (10), submarines (10), galleons (11), binoculars (11), veer boots (12), schooners (12), massive (13), koenoekoe (15)

Chapter 2 (Pages 19 to 28):

blackout (19), leeward (20), cowardly (21), mutiny (21), crude oil (21), disheartened (24), destroyer (25), bow (26), stern (26), bridge house (26), stack (26), clenched (27), massive (27)

Chapter 3 (Pages 29 to 39):

torpedoed (29), sextant (30), lubricating (30), ignited (30), haunches (31), alabaster (32), trench (32), welt (32), calypso (33), ebony (33), alligatored (33), cleats (34), despair (34), flimsy (34), outrageous (36), remote (36), secured (36), keg (36), defiantly (37), papayas (37), deftly (38)

Chapter 4 (Pages 41 to 48):

aimlessly (41), outrageous (42)

Chapter 5 (Pages 49 to 53):

port (50), harass (50), scanning (51), meliss (molest) (51), massive (52)

Chapter 6 (Pages 55 to 58):

harassment (56)

Chapter 7 (Pages 59 to 65):

cay (60), langosta (60)

Chapter 8 (Pages 67 to 72):

fronds (67), scorpions (69)

Chapter 9 (Pages 73 to 76):

reeve

THE CAY
BY THEODORE TAYLOR

Chapter 10 (Pages 77 to 82):

catchment (77), steel bands (79), pompano (80), rancid (80), sea grape (80), vaguely (82)

Chapter 11 (Pages 83 to 91):

melon (83), submerged (84), d'jumbi (85), voodoo (85), conniving (86), tethered (88), kin (89), skate (89)

Chapter 12 (Pages 93 to 96):

malaria (93)

Chapter 13 (Pages 97 to 104):

treacherous (98), crevices (98), stobs (100)

Chapter 14 (Pages 105 to 109):

calico (105), scallops (105), hurricane (106)

Chapter 15 (Pages 111 to 117):

surf (112), slithering (112), receded (113), flayed (116)

Chapter 16 (Pages 119 to 125):

groped (119), cellophane (120), bung (120), debris (120), legacy (122), precis (123), muted (125)

Chapter 17 (Pages 127 to 130):

flailing (130), gingerly (130), moray eel (130)

Chapter 18 (Pages 131 to 138):

smudge (134), sulphur (136)

Chapter 19 (Pages 139 to 144):

badgering (141), priority (141)

Suggestions for Vocabulary Activities

1. **Puzzles and Word Searches**:

   The students should be encouraged to make puzzles using the vocabulary words. They probably could work individually or in groups. The children then could exchange the puzzles and try to solve them.

2. **Vocabulary Bee**:

   This activity is similar to a spelling bee. The students probably will not be expected to spell every word correctly, but they should be able to give the correct definition.

3. **Vocabulary Charades**:

   The students are given a vocabulary word to act out while the rest of the class tries to guess which word was portrayed.

4. **Pictionary**:

   The students take turns drawing the assigned vocabulary word while the rest of the class tries to guess what has been illustrated.

5. **Short Stories**:

   The class is divided into groups. Each group creates a short story using all the vocabulary words given to it. The stories can be comical or serious.

6. **Sentence Challenge**:

   The students are challenged to create one sentence using as many vocabulary words as possible.

7. **Vocabulary Bingo**:

   The children are given a bingo card which has a prepared grid. The children put a vocabulary word in each space on the grid in any order but no word may be repeated. The definitions are randomly given for the words at which time the students will cover the word which has the correct definition. A winner is declared when a row of words is covered.

THE CAY

BY THEODORE TAYLOR

NAME: _____

Chapters One and Two

1. Why wasn't Phillip frightened by the war?

    _____

    _____

2. From where had the submarines come?

    _____

    _____

3. Phillip's father was not actively fighting in the war as a soldier, but his work was important in the war effort. Explain about his job.

    _____

    _____

4. Oil was a valuable material during wartime. Explain why you think this is a true statement.

    _____

    _____

5. Phillip's parents had a disagreement. What was it about and what caused it to start?

    _____

    _____

6. Why did Mother insist that she and Phillip return to the United States?

    _____

    _____

7. Why was it important to keep the refinery open?

    _____

    _____

8. Why did the submarines present a real threat to islands such as Curacao?

    _____

    _____

9. How was water obtained in the West Indies?

    _____

    _____

10. Why wasn't there enough food and water on the island?

    _____

    _____

11. What made Phillip begin to change his ideas about war?

    _____

    _____

12. Using the T-diagram, compare Phillip's father and mother.

Father	Mother

Map Work:

The story takes place in the area of the world called the Caribbean Sea. Using an atlas, put the following places on the outline map below. You can label more places if you want.

- Curacao
- Aruba
- Venezuela
- North America
- Bonaire
- South America
- Willenstad
- Florida
- Caribbean Sea
- Netherland Antilles

THE CAY
BY THEODORE TAYLOR

Crossword Puzzle

Find the words to solve the crossword puzzle from the word bank below. The puzzle clues are at the side of the page.

schooners	diesel	binoculars	massive
blackout	mutiny	pontoon bridge	stack
leeward	ballast	stern	clenched
cowardly	veerboots	koenoekoe	bow

Across:

4. countryside
5. something heavy carried in a ship to steady it
6. lacks courage or is afraid
8. the hind part of a ship or boat
10. field glasses for both eyes
11. forward part of a ship
12. ferry boats
13. a type of engine that burns crude oil
14. open rebellion against authority
15. chimney

Down:

1. closed
2. in the direction toward which the wind is blowing
3. a bridge supported on pontoons
7. darken completely
8. ships with two or more masts and sails set lengthwise
9. big and heavy; large and solid

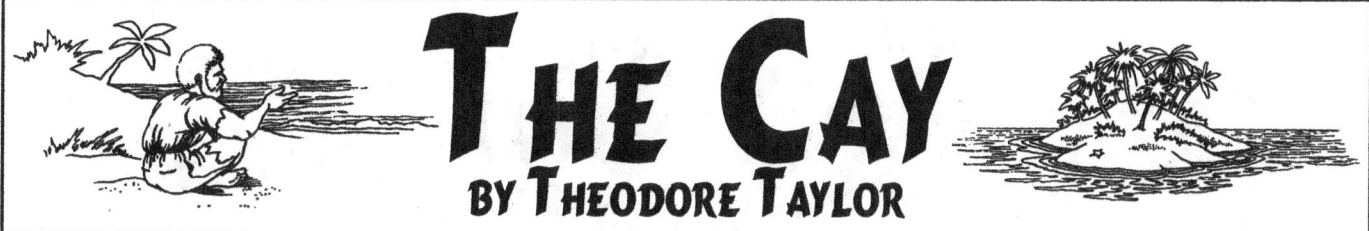

Chapter Three

1. In a short paragraph, write a description of what happened to the ship.

   _____
   _____
   _____
   _____

2. Why do you suppose Phillip's mother was "different" after the torpedoing?

   _____
   _____

3. How was Phillip saved?

   _____
   _____

4. Describe the colored man on the lines below and make a sketch of him.

   _____
   _____
   _____
   _____
   _____
   _____
   _____
   _____

5. Why wouldn't Phillip eat?

   _____
   _____

6. Why did Phillip have a headache?

   _____
   _____

7. How did they "catch" the fish?

   _____
   _____

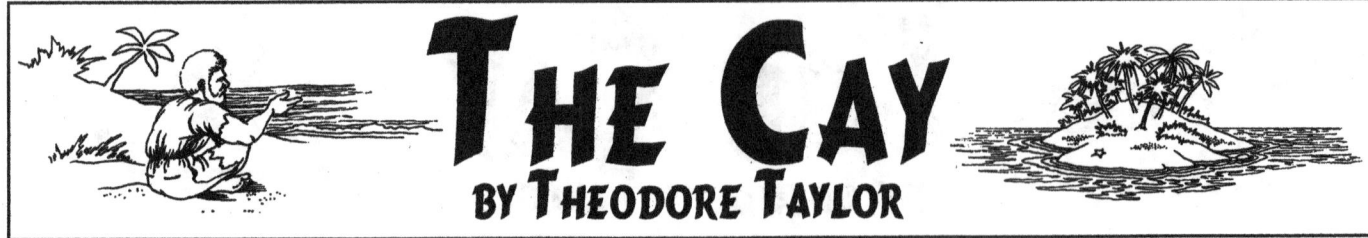

THE CAY
BY THEODORE TAYLOR

8. Make a sketch of the sailing ship (raft with its crude sails). Write a short description on the lines.

_____
_____
_____
_____
_____
_____
_____

9. Why did the water have to be "rationed" carefully?

_____
_____

10. "Prejudice" comes into this chapter. Explain what this word means.

_____
_____

11. Using the web below, brainstorm with a partner to discover the term "prejudice".

Antonym

in favour of
_____
_____
_____

Synonym

dislike
_____
_____
_____

Prejudice

Definition In Own Words

what does the word mean
_____
_____
_____

Related To Experience

e.g. an experience you've had with this feeling
_____
_____
_____

Chapter Four

1. When darkness came, what two things caused the survivors on the raft to be cold?
   a) _____
   b) _____

2. Why did Phillip "draw back" when his body touched Timothy's?
   _____
   _____

3. Why do you think Stew Cat is important?
   _____
   _____

4. What made Phillip think that Timothy came from Africa?
   _____
   _____

5. What terribly frightening thing happened in this chapter?
   _____
   _____

6. How did Phillip react to his blindness?
   _____
   _____

7. Predict what the new conflicts in the story will be?
   _____
   _____

8. Illustrate a scene from the chapter.

Chapter Five

1. If you were to survive on a raft out at sea, what six items would you need? Make a list below.

   _____   _____
   _____   _____
   _____   _____

2. What did Timothy mean when he said, "motah"?

   _____

3. How did Timothy make a torch? Sketch how you think it looked.

   _____
   _____
   _____
   _____

4. Why was it so dangerous to fall into the water?

   _____
   _____

5. How do you know Timothy is superstitious? What is meant by superstition?

   _____
   _____
   _____

6. What is a "booby"?

   _____
   _____

7. Timothy speaks in a dialect that is not the same as English. What is a "dialect"?

   _____
   _____

8. List some phrases below that Timothy uses and try to explain what they mean.

   Unusual Phrase   **Possible Pronunciation**

   _____   _____
   _____   _____
   _____   _____
   _____   _____
   _____   _____

Chapter Six

1. What caused Phillip to fall overboard?

   _____

   _____

2. What made Timothy so angry?

   _____

   _____

3. What did Timothy see that raised his spirits?

   _____

   _____

4. Why didn't Phillip want to go onto the island?

   _____

   _____

5. Make a prediction: How big is the island? _____

   What are they going to discover? _____

   _____

   Who will they find? _____

   _____

6. Use the following story starter to write an underwater adventure story.

Underwater Adventure

I was lying quietly on the raft when suddenly it lurched and I fell in the water...

THE CAY
BY THEODORE TAYLOR

Chapter Seven

1. Why did Timothy jump into the water?
   _____
   _____

2. Why didn't Timothy seem afraid of sharks?
   _____
   _____

3. In the space, make a sketch and explain about the "langosta".

   _____
   _____
   _____
   _____
   _____
   _____

4. Phillip felt Timothy was "holding back" (page 62). Explain what he meant.
   _____
   _____

5. What made Phillip so frightened?
   _____
   _____

6. From Timothy's rough calculations, how big is the island?
   _____
   _____

7. Why did Phillip feel it was a mistake to have landed on this island? List the reasons.
   a) _____
   b) _____
   c) _____

8. On the outline sketch of the island, add the things that Timothy found on the island.

Chapter Eight

1. Why might there not be a search party out looking for the two survivors?

   _____

   _____

2. Why was Phillip afraid to be alone?

   _____

   _____

3. How did Stew Cat comfort Phillip?

   _____

   _____

4. In this chapter, you learn several different things about Timothy. List them below.

   a) _____

   b) _____

   c) _____

   d) _____

5. If Timothy and Phillip are to survive on the Cay, what will they have to do? Work cooperatively with a partner and list your ideas on the noticeboard below.

Survival on the Cay

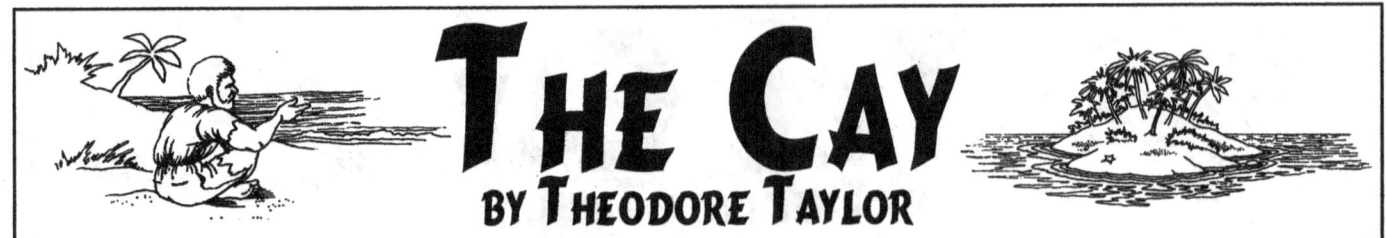

THE CAY
BY THEODORE TAYLOR

Island Rhyme Rescue

Find the words in the chapter that rhyme with each of the words below.

1. fried _____ (67)

2. bonds _____ (67)

3. calm _____ (67)

4. wire _____ (67)

5. damp _____ (67)

6. found _____ (68)

7. sleeve _____ (68)

8. kind _____ (69)

9. mobster _____ (69)

10. reach _____ (70)

11. unite _____ (70)

12. sprawled _____ (70)

13. moaned _____ (71)

14. interior _____ (72)

15. tick _____ (72)

True or False

1.   T   F   When Phillip fell in the water, he was bitten by a shark.

2.   T   F   Timothy saved Phillip.

3.   T   F   The raft was a safe place from sharks.

4.   T   F   The cay is a large island inhabited by many people.

5.   T   F   Phillip helped Timothy build a hut.

6.   T   F   Phillip fished for langosta for supper.

7.   T   F   Phillip was afraid to be left alone.

8.   T   F   Stew Cat was a faithful companion for Phillip.

9.   T   F   Timothy was twenty years old.

10.   T   F   S O S was written in the sand.

11.   T   F   A signal fire will surely attract an airplane.

12.   T   F   Phillip discovered that Timothy could not read.

Chapters Nine and Ten

1. What was the purpose of the rope?

   _____

   _____

2. How did Timothy expect Phillip to help?

   _____

3. How did Phillip begin to change?

   _____

   _____

4. Do you think they would have become friends if Timothy had not slapped Phillip? Why?

   _____

   _____

5. Give two reasons why they were glad to have rain.
   a) _____
   b) _____

6. Why did Phillip want the rain to continue?

   _____

   _____

7. Using the Venn Diagram, compare and contrast Timothy and Phillip's childhood.

Timothy   **Phillip**

Vocabulary Practice

Match the words with the meanings.

1. catchment   _____ fastened by rope, chain or thong

2. pompano   _____ leaf-like shoot of a palm tree

3. rancid   _____ small, round sea animals with sharp spines

4. steel bands   _____ indefinitely, uncertainty

5. fronds   _____ musical instruments

6. scorpions   _____ small islet composed of sand and coral

7. reeve   _____ trough to catch and funnel water into a container

8. vaguely   _____ kind of fish

9. cay   _____ native lobster without claws

10. langosta   _____ stale

11. sea urchins   _____ poisonous arachnid

12. tethered   _____ pass in or through something

Make your own HELP sign below.

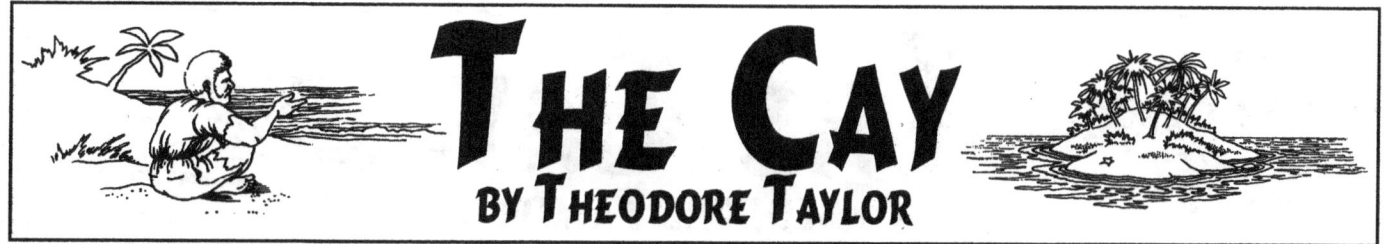

THE CAY
BY THEODORE TAYLOR

Creative Work: Mental Images

From the basic outline below, add features:

- the hut
- the rain catchment
- HELP sign

- the palm trees
- the vine
- the rescue fire

- the beach
- the rope leading to the beach

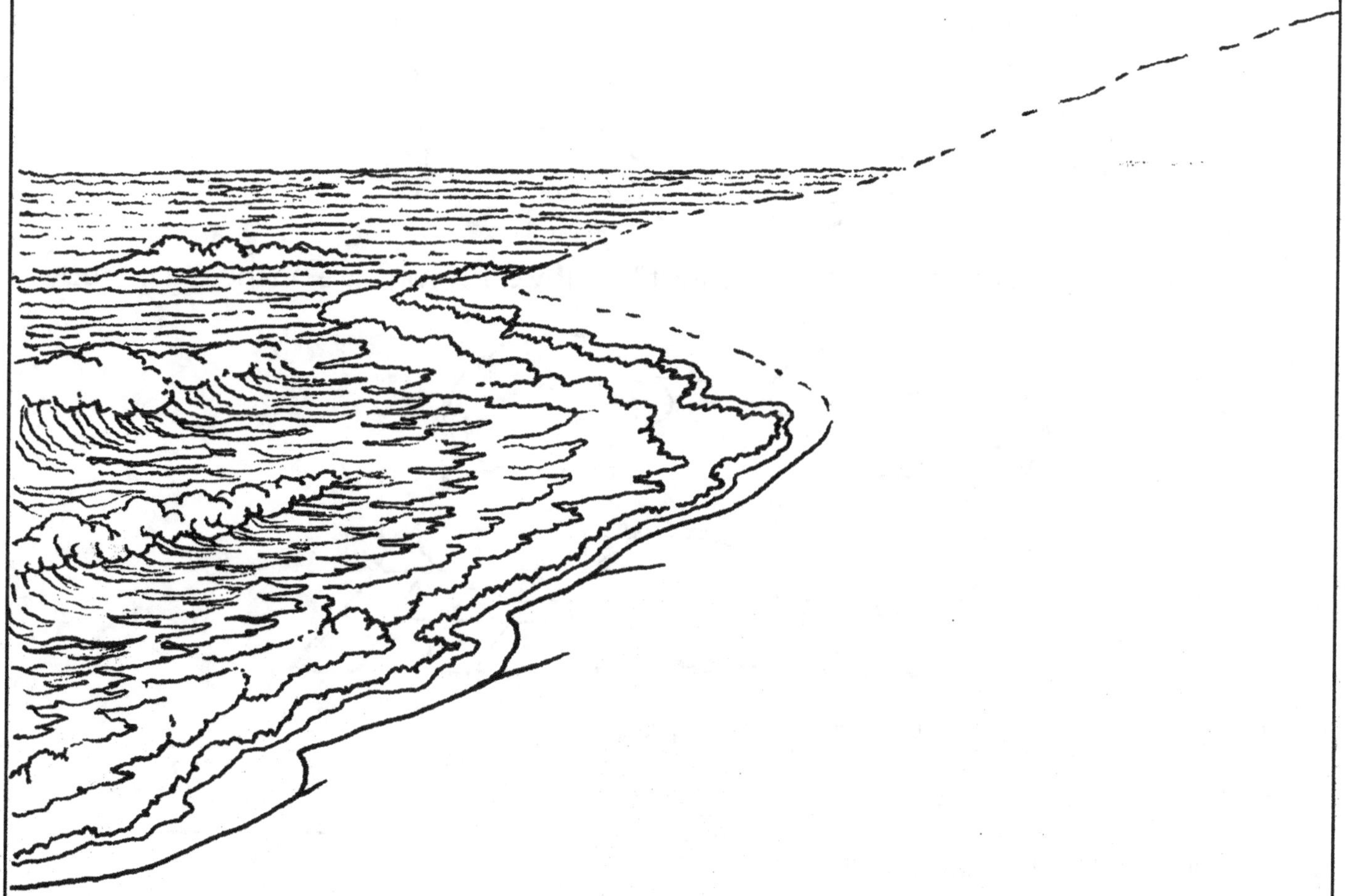

Chapter Eleven

1. Using the table place setting, add foods on the plate that you like to eat.

2. Now on the rough matt, place the foods that Timothy and Phillip ate on the Cay. Study page 80.

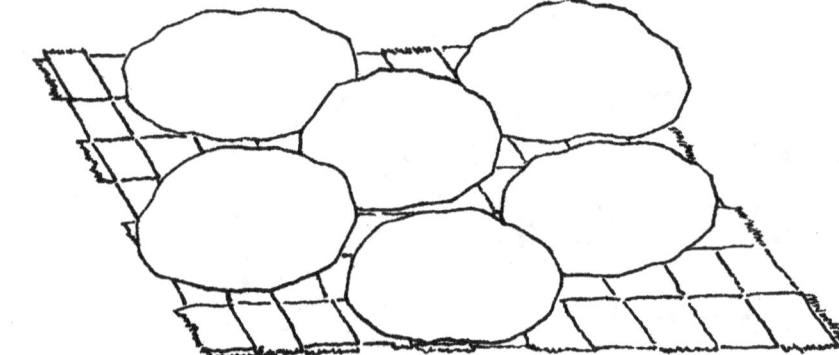

3. Why did Timothy try to make Phillip independent?

_____

_____

4. Why did Timothy think Stew Cat is "d'jumbi"?

_____

_____

5. What things did Timothy do that made Phillip suspicious of what he had done to Stew Cat?

_____

_____

6. In what ways could Phillip have had a dangerous experience when he went out in the water?

_____

_____

7. In the space provided, relate a time when you have lost a pet or your pet has been injured. Make a portrait of your pet.

MY PET

_____
_____
_____
_____
_____
_____
_____
_____
_____
_____
_____
_____
_____
_____

Chapter Twelve

1. What made Timothy run a fever?

   _____

   _____

2. List the things Phillip did for Timothy.
   a) _____
   b) _____
   c) _____
   d) _____

3. Why did Timothy run into the water?

   _____

4. Why was the delirious state dangerous for both Phillip and Timothy?

   _____

   _____

5. Predict what you think the sentence means about what will happen in the future: "He never really regained his strength."

   _____

   _____

6. Research the topic "Cays". Explain how Cays develop (page 101) or using other reference materials.

CAYS

_____
_____
_____
_____
_____
_____
_____
_____
_____
_____
_____
_____
_____
_____
_____

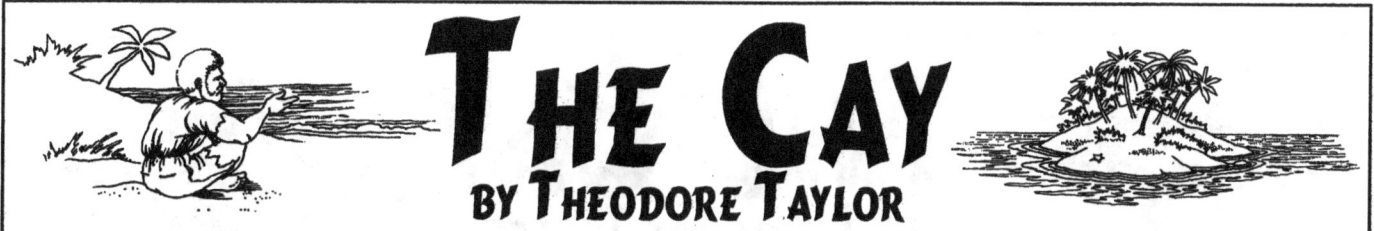

THE CAY
BY THEODORE TAYLOR

Chapter Thirteen

1. How did Phillip keep track of the date?

   _____

   _____

2. Why is it necessary for Phillip to learn how to fish?

   _____

   _____

3. What was used for fishhooks?

   _____

4. From the description on page 98, make a sketch of the fishing hole.

5. Why did they need to catch a mussel first?

   _____

   _____

6. Why does fishing now feel so special for Phillip?

   _____

   _____

7. List the ways Phillip is maturing as described in this chapter.

   a) _____

   b) _____

   c) _____

   d) _____

8. What do you think Phillip meant when he said, "Timothy, are you still black?"?

   _____

   _____

THE CAY
BY THEODORE TAYLOR

Chapter 14 (Pages 105 to 109)

1. What made the noise like a rifle?

   _____

   _____

2. Why did the sound frighten Timothy?

   _____

   _____

3. List the other signals that proved to Timothy that a hurricane was coming.

   a) _____

   b) _____

   c) _____

4. List the preparations that Timothy made as the storm approached.

   _____

   _____

   _____

5. Research: Find the difference between:

   a) hurricane watch _____

   b) hurricane warning_____

   c) hurricane alert _____

6. On the outline sketch of the Cay, show how Timothy and Phillip protected themselves during the storm.

Storm Protection

THE CAY

BY THEODORE TAYLOR

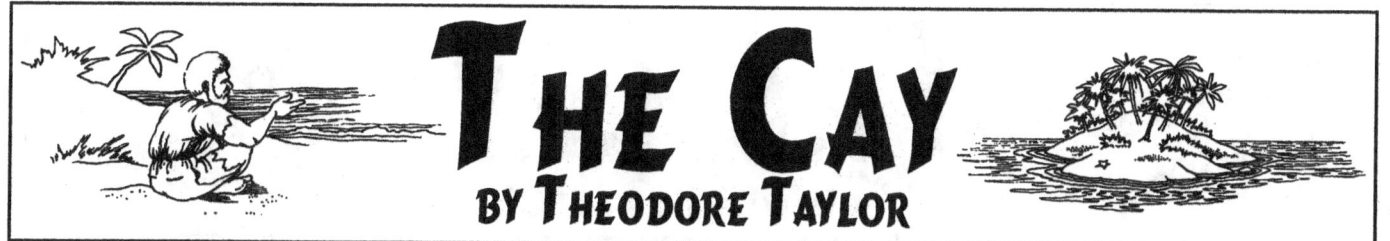

7. Using the Triple Venn graphic organizer, record your findings on the similarities and differences of the types of storms mentioned.

Storms

Hurricane **Tornado**

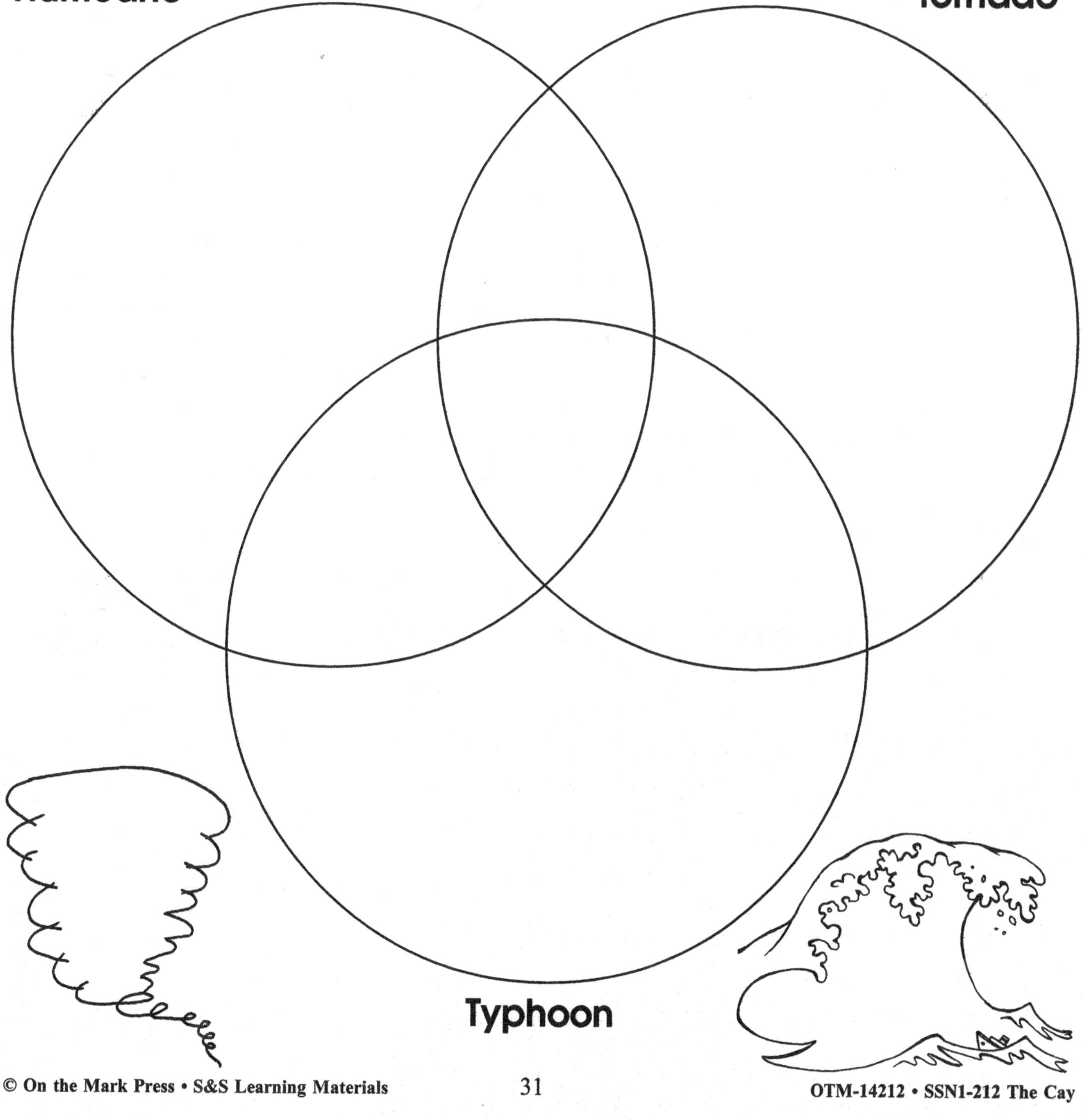

Typhoon

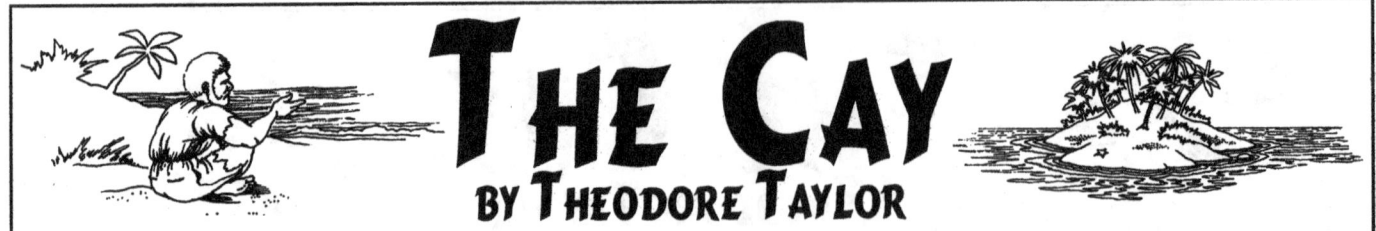

THE CAY
BY THEODORE TAYLOR

Chapter Fifteen

1. Explain how the appearance of the sky changed.

   _____

   _____

2. Study page 113 to discover how high the waves and the sea had risen.

   _____

   _____

3. Why was Phillip shivering (page 112)?

   _____

   _____

4. Tell three things that happened to show how strong the wind had become.
   a) _____
   b) _____
   c) _____

5. How did Timothy save them from being blown away by the hurricane?

   _____

   _____

6. Why was there a calm time for about twenty to thirty minutes?

   _____

   _____

7. What caused Timothy's back to bleed?

   _____

   _____

8. How do you suppose Stew Cat survived the hurricane? Explain.

   _____

   _____

9. What happened at the end of the chapter to sadden Phillip?

   _____

   _____

10. List the words you can find in the novel that would best describe Timothy.

   _____   _____   _____

   _____   _____   _____

11. What small, happy event comforted Phillip?

   _____

   _____

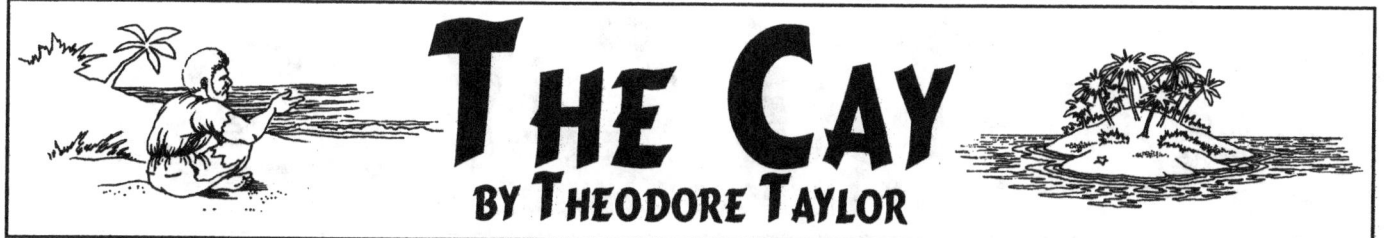

Hurricane Poetry

Cinquain Poem (Poem of five lines)

1. Line 1   Write "Hurricane".
2. Line 2   Describing words for hurricane.
3. Line 3   Three words that give action to the hurricane.
4. Line 4   Four words that express feelings about hurricanes.
5. Line 5   One word that refers to the title (another word)

Chapter Sixteen

1. What does "littered with debris" mean on page 120?

   _____

   _____

2. What do you think Phillip meant when he said, "I also think that had I been able to see, I might not have been able to accept it all" (page 119)?

   _____

   _____

3. Contemplate why Timothy trained Phillip very carefully and explain (page 121).

   _____

   _____

4. On the chart below, explain how Phillip discovered the Cay was recovering after the storm.

Landscape	Signal Fire	Water	Food	Shelter
a) _____				
b) _____				
c) _____				
d) _____				

5. Record the things Phillip found as he explored the island.

   _____

   _____

   _____

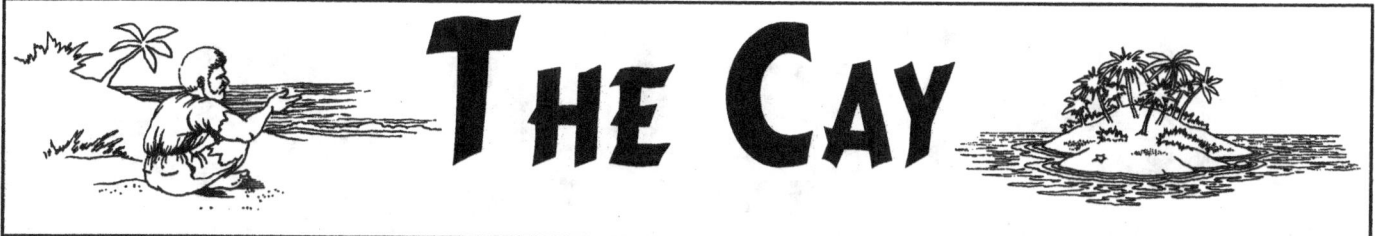

6. Distinguish in what ways Phillip was like the birds.

   _____

   _____

7. On the outline sheet at the end of the booklet, consider what it would be like for you to be alone and blind on the Cay. Explain about what you would fear the most and your thoughts about your future.

8. Phillip had a mental image of where everything was on the island. Create a map to share with a classmate.

   PHILLIP'S ISLAND

9. Design a grave stone for Timothy.

   Remember: Phillip has limited materials and he is blind, but he wants to remember where Timothy is buried.

Chapter Seventeen

1. Why do you think the statement, "If I'm not out in twenty minutes, you better jump in and get me" is humorous?

   _____

   _____

2. Explain why Phillip decided to stop eating coconuts.

   _____

   _____

3. Why couldn't Phillip obtain scallops?

   _____

   _____

4. Why did Phillip decide to go in the "fishing hole"?

   _____

   _____

5. As indicated in the story, in what ways was Phillip safe in the fishing hole from the following:

   sharks: _____

   _____

   barracuda _____

   _____

   octopus _____

   _____

6. Action Story: At the Fishing Hole

   In the shapes provided, relate the episode of the incident at the bottom of the fishing hole. Be sure to divide the action into four equal parts and explain each event in a detailed sentence.

ACTION STORY
AT THE
FISHING HOLE

THE CAY
BY THEODORE TAYLOR

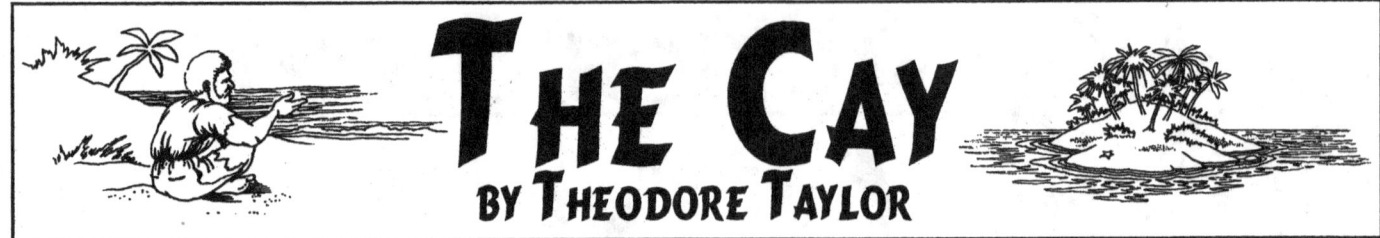

Chapter Eighteen

1. How was Phillip able to achieve the dark smoke to attract the airplane?

2. When people are blind, they develop other ways for a visual image of the world around them. On the chart below, use words from the chapter to explain what Phillip used to explain the sounds in the left column.

birds

breeze

Stew Cat

airplane

signal fire

3. Why did the chance of Phillip's rescue seem hopeless?

4. What do you suppose would have happened if Timothy have lived or if Phillip had not been blind?

Chapter Nineteen

1. As Phillip moved toward his rescuer, the man gasped, "Are you blind?". How do you suppose he made that observation?

   _____

   _____

2. Why would the people Phillip spoke to have trouble understanding what happened on the Cay?

   _____

   _____

3. How do you suppose Phillip's mother changed?

   _____

   _____

4. Remember: Complete the attribute webs. There have been changes to both Phillip and his mother.

5. On the comparison chart, show how Phillip is like you and is different from you.

Phillip	**You**
_____	_____
_____	_____
_____	_____
_____	_____
_____	_____
_____	_____
_____	_____
_____	_____
_____	_____
_____	_____

6. Choose the part of the story that you found the most frightening. Use the next page to illustrate that part and explain about why you think it was so tense.

MOST FRIGHTENING PART

THE CAY
BY THEODORE TAYLOR

Extra Activities: Masterpiece Creations

WET CHALK AND PAINT DESIGNS

Materials:
- colored chalks
- tempera paint
- manilla drawing paper
- large flat pan of water (cookie sheet)

Directions:

1. On separate manilla drawing paper, draw Timothy and Phillip tied to the palm tree during the hurricane. Show them surrounded by water and show the strong wind. Color the picture with colored chalks.

2. After the drawing is done, completely immerse the paper in the flat pan of water.

3. Remove the wet drawing from the pan, place on a smooth flat surface and sprinkle small amounts of different colored tempera paint on the surface. Use a brush to blend colors.

4. While the paper is still wet, use the colored chalks to outline the picture if it has become faint or smudged.

5. Set it to dry. Display it in the classroom or in the hallway.

BOOK JACKET

Create a new book cover for the novel.

Materials:
- manilla drawing paper 23 cm x 30 cm (9" x 12")
- pencils, crayons or felt markers

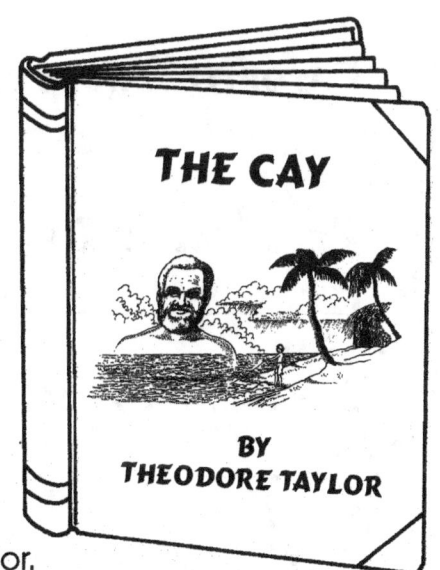

Directions:

1. Fold the drawing paper in half.

2. Make colorful illustrations on the front cover.

3. On the back cover, print praise comments that have been made by other readers.

4. Inside the front cover, draw a memorable picture from the novel.

5. On the inside back cover, prepare a biography of the author.

WANTED POSTER

Create a wanted poster for Phillip.

WANTED

PHILLIP

AGE: _____

PHYSICAL DESCRIPTION: _____

_____

FAVORITE THOUGHTS: _____

_____

PERSONALITY DESCRIPTION: _____

_____

SPECIAL FRIENDS: _____

STORY MAPPING

Show the story in five important parts. Write a sentence about each part.

1. _____
   _____

2. _____
   _____

3. _____
   _____

4. _____
   _____

5. _____
   _____

SEQUENCE OF EVENTS

Below are a list of the important events in the story.

Number the events in order to show when they took place.

_____ Timothy makes a hut for a shelter on the Cay.

_____ The ship, the Hato, with Phillip and his mother aboard is torpedoed.

_____ A hurricane blows across the Cay destroying the hut.

_____ Phillip is rescued by a small boat.

_____ Phillip discovers that he is blind.

_____ Phillip is bitten by a moray eel.

_____ Timothy dies leaving Phillip and Stew Cat alone on the Cay.

_____ Phillip and Henrik watch the excitement of the war on Curacao.

_____ Timothy makes a vine rope that leads to the signal fire on the beach.

_____ Phillip is reunited with his parents.

_____ Phillip stumbles off the raft and into the shark infested water.

_____ Timothy teaches Phillip to fish in the fishing hole.

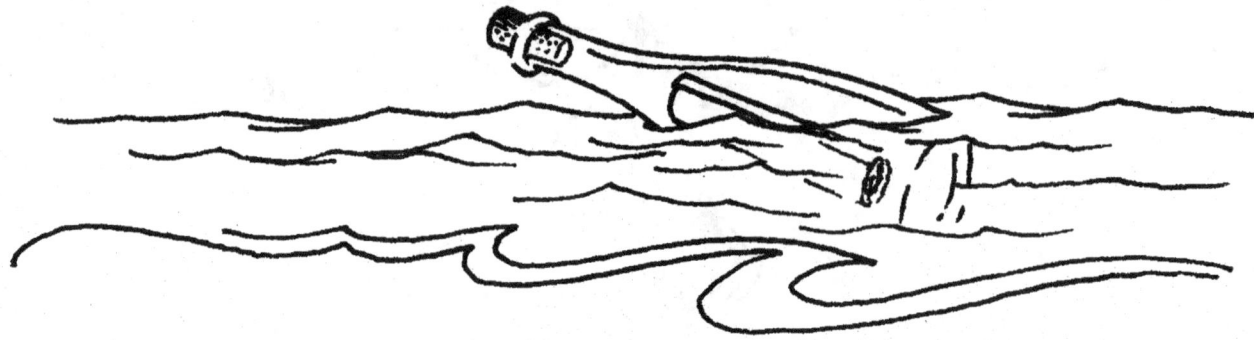

WORD SEARCH

P	O	R	T	M	O	R	A	Y	E	E	L	P	V
N	R	S	N	O	I	P	R	O	C	S	A	C	E
F	T	R	E	N	C	H	W	L	A	R	O	C	E
R	A	N	C	I	D	U	E	L	T	O	N	M	R
O	B	E	T	S	R	A	L	U	C	O	N	I	B
N	O	D	E	P	R	O	T	B	H	D	Y	E	O
D	U	A	L	W	O	N	A	P	M	O	P	B	O
S	I	G	N	A	L	F	I	R	E	O	T	O	T
G	M	N	K	S	T	E	R	N	N	V	S	N	S
S	A	U	B	A	L	L	A	S	T	D	H	Y	G
T	R	B	D	K	I	Y	L	E	E	W	A	R	D
O	O	P	L	G	E	N	A	C	I	R	R	U	H
B	O	W	S	H	E	Y	M	C	T	P	K	I	N
S	N	I	H	C	R	U	A	E	S	T	A	C	K

Words to Find:

CAY	BINOCULARS	CATCHMENT	POMPANO	SCORPIONS
PORT	TORPEDO	SHARK	HURRICANE	EBONY
LEEWARD	VEERBOOTS	MALARIA	TRENCH	SIGNAL FIRE
FRONDS	SMUDGE	BOW	BUNG	BALLAST
WELT	CORAL	RANCID	VOODOO	SEA URCHINS
STOBS	STERN	STACK	MAROON	MORAY EEL

Unscramble the outlined letters to make two words:

The words are: _____

What do the two words mean? Check page 101 of the novel. _____

_____

Phillip's Return to the Cay

Think ahead in the future to a time when Phillip is a grown man. When he left the cay, he vowed that he would return one day. Suppose that when he returned he took his mother and father. What do you think he would want to share with them about his experience.

Write an account of Phillip's trip and what he did when he landed on the cay. Remember this time he **can see** all the sights.

_____

_____

_____

_____

_____

_____

_____

_____

_____

_____

_____

_____

_____

_____

_____

_____

EXTRA! EXTRA! READ ALL ABOUT IT!

NEWSPAPER STORY

Prepare a newspaper story that you can present to the class.

Remember:

- Create a headline. Should be short and to the point.
  Example: Boy Rescued From Cay

- Explain the events that caused the rescue to take place.
  Example: signal fire, airplane, boat.

- Phillip's physical and emotional condition.
  Example: blindness, suffering from malnutrition

- Phillip's companions.

- Prepare the page with the following: Headline, Picture, Written Article

PHILLIP'S ATTRIBUTE WEB

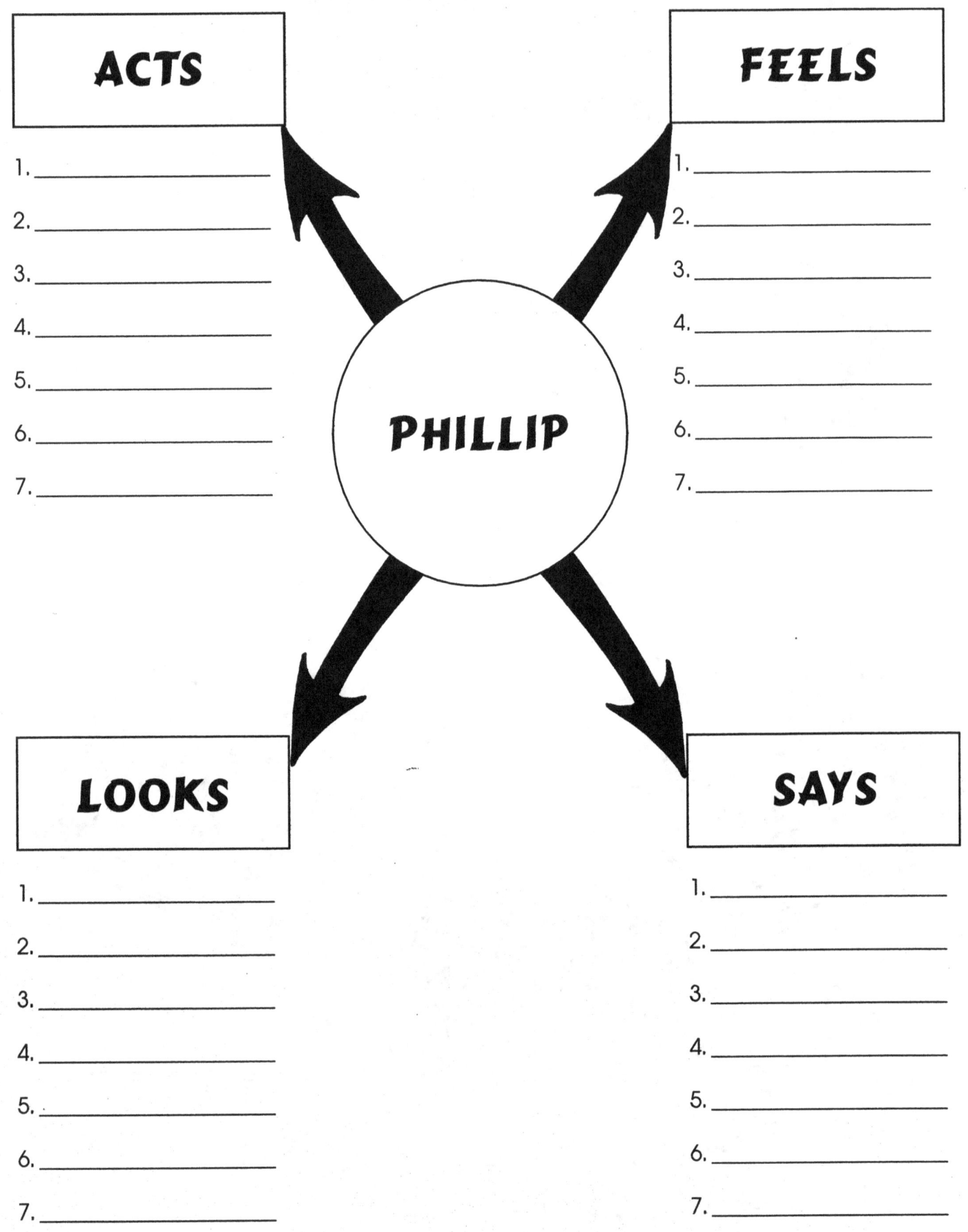

ACTS

1. _____
2. _____
3. _____
4. _____
5. _____
6. _____
7. _____

FEELS

1. _____
2. _____
3. _____
4. _____
5. _____
6. _____
7. _____

PHILLIP

LOOKS

1. _____
2. _____
3. _____
4. _____
5. _____
6. _____
7. _____

SAYS

1. _____
2. _____
3. _____
4. _____
5. _____
6. _____
7. _____

Timothy's Attribute Web

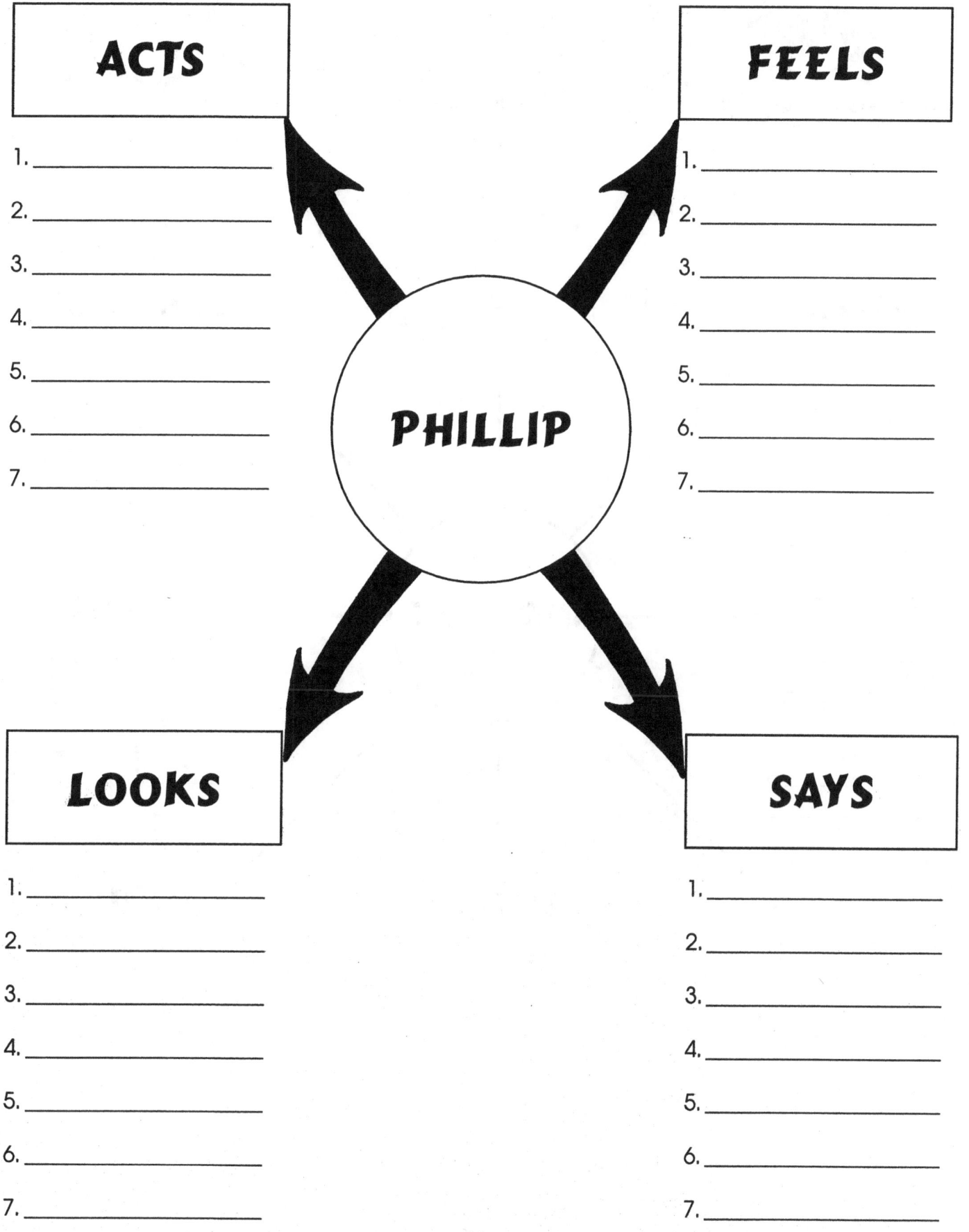

ACTS

1. _____
2. _____
3. _____
4. _____
5. _____
6. _____
7. _____

FEELS

1. _____
2. _____
3. _____
4. _____
5. _____
6. _____
7. _____

PHILLIP

LOOKS

1. _____
2. _____
3. _____
4. _____
5. _____
6. _____
7. _____

SAYS

1. _____
2. _____
3. _____
4. _____
5. _____
6. _____
7. _____

SURVIVAL WEB

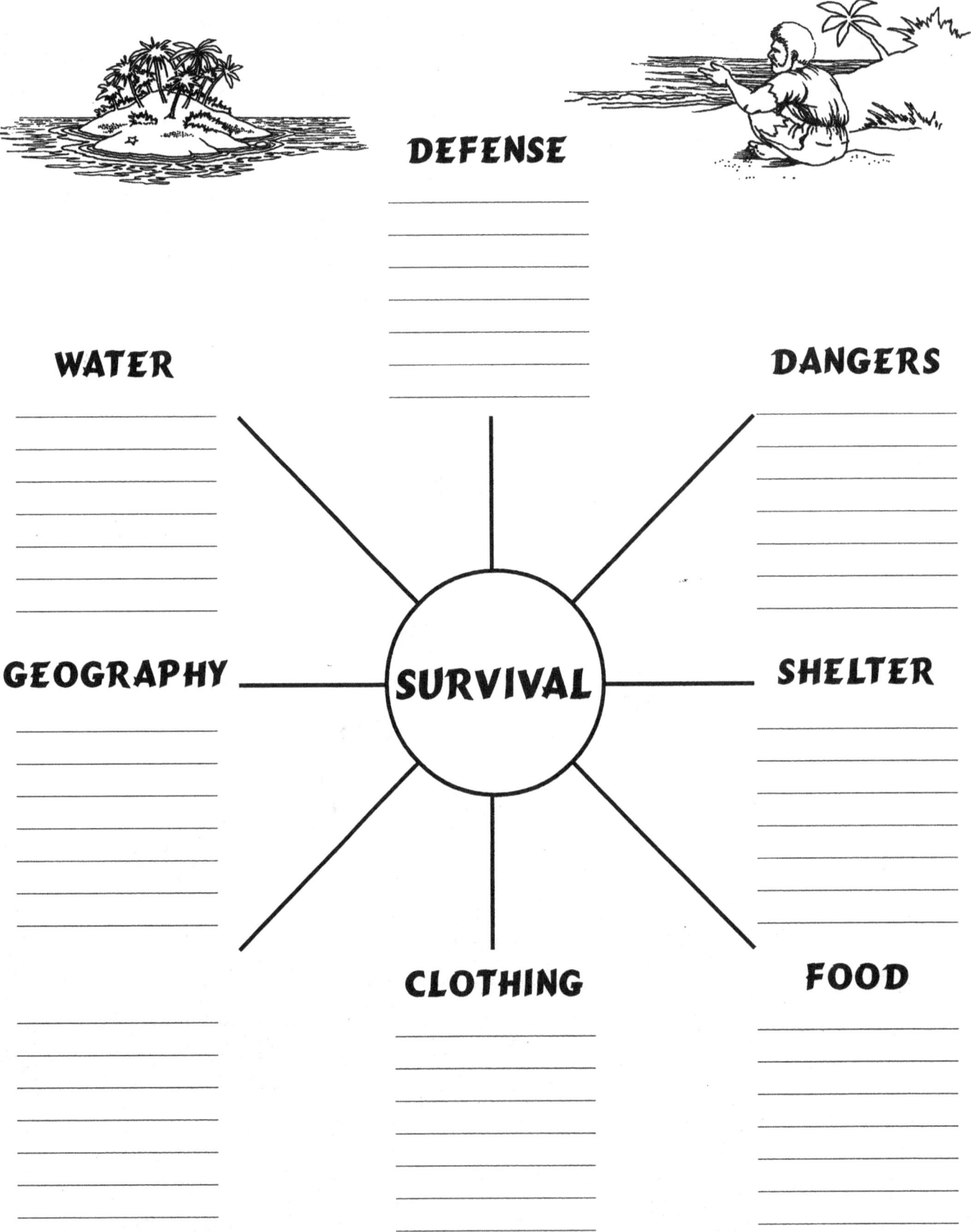

DEFENSE

WATER

DANGERS

GEOGRAPHY — SURVIVAL — SHELTER

CLOTHING

FOOD

THE CAY
BY THEODORE TAYLOR

ANALYSIS OF THE STORY

Choose parts from the story and explain in detail why you chose that part.

1. The part of the story that I found the most frightening was _____
   _____
   _____

2. The part of the story that had the most action and excitement was _____
   _____
   _____

3. The part of the story that was the saddest was _____
   _____
   _____

4. The part of the story that was the most realistic was _____
   _____
   _____

5. The part of the story that was the most meaningful was _____
   _____
   _____

6. If you could change the ending of the story, what changes would you make?
   _____
   _____
   _____

7. The character that you would like to have as a friend is _____
   Why? _____
   _____
   _____

8. On the back of this page, make a drawing of the part of the story that you liked best.

MALARIA

Plan a research paper on the topic of Malaria. Remember to answer the following questions:
- How do people get malaria?
- In what parts of the world is malaria common?
- What is the treatment for malaria?

MALARIA

_____

_____

_____

_____

_____

_____

_____

_____

_____

_____

_____

_____

_____

_____

_____

_____

_____

_____

OTM-14212 • SSN1-212 The Cay

WINNING EFFORT

Add endings to the root words to make new words.

		ed	**ing**
1.	shout	_____	_____
2.	flap	_____	_____
3.	fit	_____	_____
4.	extend	_____	_____
5.	murmur	_____	_____
6.	submerge	_____	_____
7.	drop	_____	_____
8.	protest	_____	_____
9.	smolder	_____	_____
10.	awaken	_____	_____
11.	discuss	_____	_____
12.	explode	_____	_____
13.	connive	_____	_____
14.	plan	_____	_____
15.	separate	_____	_____
16.	convince	_____	_____
17.	frighten	_____	_____
18.	echo	_____	_____
19.	salvage	_____	_____
20.	fascinate	_____	_____

MATH TO THE RESCUE

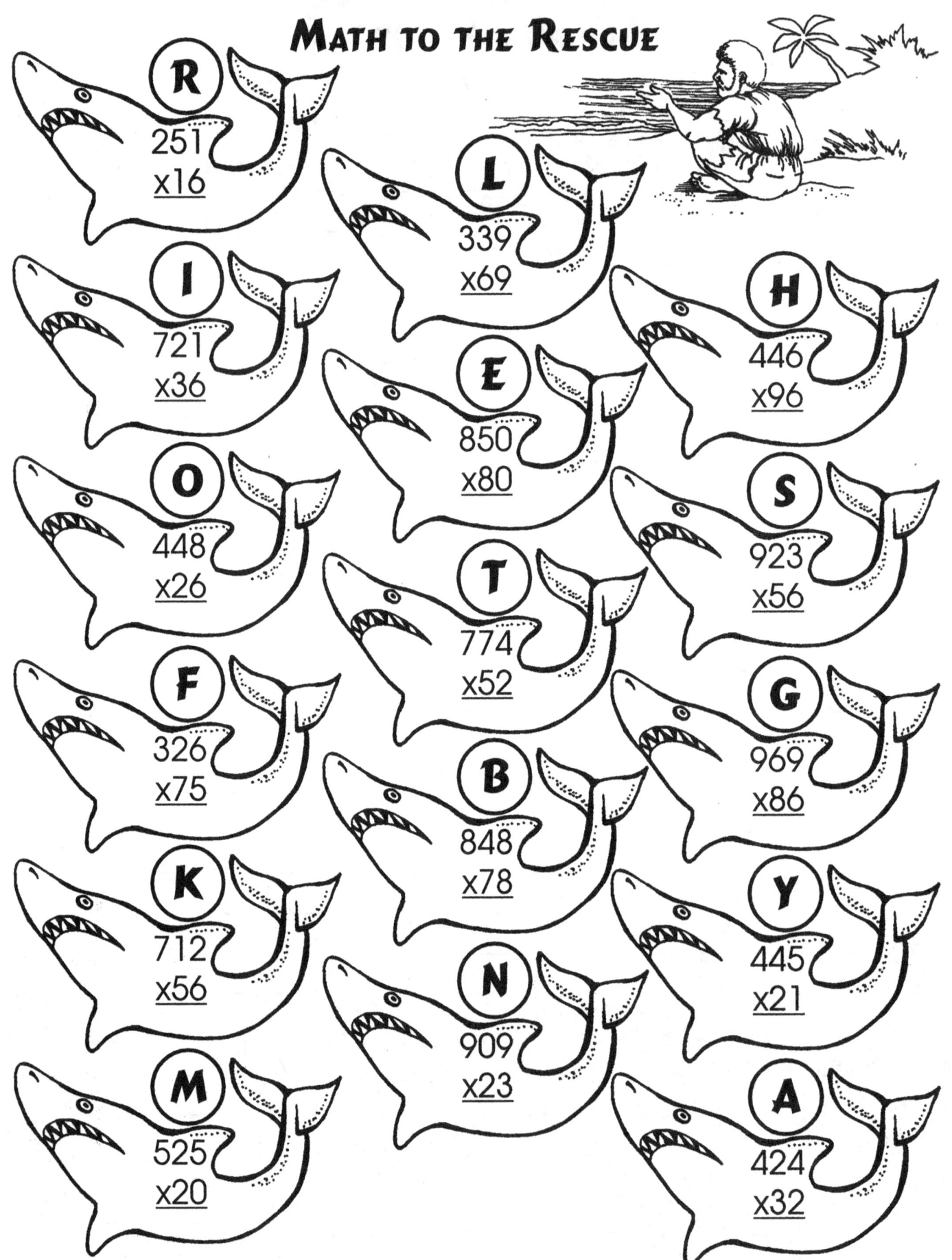

R
251
x16

I
721
x36

O
448
x26

F
326
x75

K
712
x56

M
525
x20

L
339
x69

E
850
x80

T
774
x52

B
848
x78

N
909
x23

H
446
x96

S
923
x56

G
969
x86

Y
445
x21

A
424
x32

From your answer, use the letters beside each fish to solve the coded message.

54   OTM-14212 • SSN1-212 The Cay

Secret Message

Why is a shipwrecked sailor on an abandoned island like a bargain hunter?

40,248   42,816   68,000   9,345   4,016   68,000
◯   ◯   ◯   ◯   ◯   ◯

66,144   11,648   40,248   42,816
◯   ◯   ◯   ◯

23,391   11,648   11,648   39,872   25,956   20,907   83,334
◯   ◯   ◯   ◯   ◯   ◯   ◯

24,450   11,648   4,016
◯   ◯   ◯

13,568
◯

51,688   13,568   23,391   68,000
◯   ◯   ◯   ◯

Answer Key

Chapters One and Two:

1. Paul wasn't frightened, but terribly excited. It was something he had heard a lot about but had never seen.
2. The submarines came from Germany.
3. Phillip's father worked in the refinery. He worked on the program to increase production of aviation gas.
4. Oil was a valuable material during wartime because oil and gasoline are needed for the machinery (tanks, trucks, jeeps, ships) that are used to fight the war.
5. Phillip's parents argued about living in Curacao. She didn't like the smell of gas and oil and she felt it was unsafe living in Curacao.
6. Mother insisted that she and Phillip return to the United States because it was too dangerous in Curacao.
7. It was important to keep the refinery open because precious gas and oil could not get to England or to the war in the African desert.
8. The submarines presented a real threat to islands such as Curacao because the tankers from the United States were held in port so they couldn't get water or fresh vegetables.
9. Water was brought by big tankers from the United States or England.
10. There wasn't enough food and water on the island because the schooner-men were not leaving their ports until the submarines were chased away.
11. Phillip was no longer excited about the war when he saw the Tern explode in flames by a German submarine.

Crossword

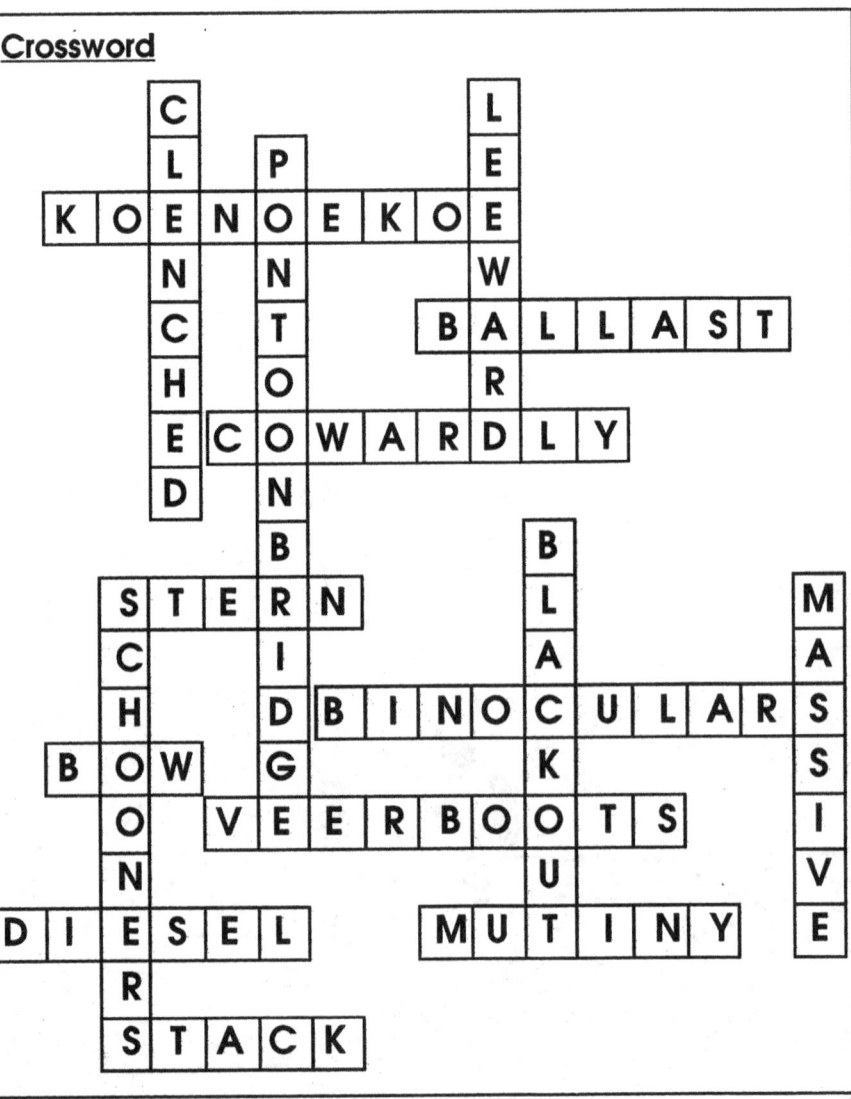

THE CAY
BY THEODORE TAYLOR

Chapter Three:
1. Ideas pages 29 and 30.
2. (Page 29) Mother was very calm but shaking. (Mother could have been suffering from shock.)
3. Phillip was saved by a very old Negro (page 31).
4. Describe the colored man (pages 31-33).
5. Phillip wouldn't eat because the fish was raw.
6. Phillip had a headache because something had hit him on the side of the head when they were leaving the sinking ship.
7. Description page 34.
8. The flying fish flopped on the raft.
9. Water had to be rationed carefully because they must make it last. They cannot drink salt water from the ocean.
10. Prejudice means a judgment or opinion formed before the facts are known; hatred of or dislike for a particular group, race, religion.

Chapter Four:
1. Two things that caused the survivors on the raft to be cold:
   a) Darkness blotted out the sea.
   b) The wind picked up.
2. Phillip drew back faster because he could remember in Virginia they'd always lived in their section of town, and we in ours.
3. Stew Cat is important because he comforted him.
4. Phillip thinks Timothy came from Africa because he didn't know his own age.
5. The terribly frightening thing that happened was he lost his eyesight.
6. He began to crawl screaming for his mother and father. He was so frightened it was hard for him to breathe. At one point he even felt angry.
7. New conflicts - variety of answers.

Chapter Five:
1. Variety of answers.
2. By the "motah" Timothy meant motor. It could be an engine sound from a boat or plane.
3. Torch pages 49 and 50.
4. It was dangerous to fall into the water because of sharks.
5. Timothy is superstitious because he felt the cat was bad luck.
6. A "booby" is the name for bird.
7. The dialect Timothy speaks is a "southern black American dialect."
8. Variety of answers.

Chapter Six:

1. Phillip fell overboard because he was excited when Timothy shouted, "I see an island, true."
2. Timothy was angry because Phillip could have been eaten by a shark.
3. Timothy's spirits rose because he saw an island.
4. Phillip didn't want to go onto the island because he thought the planes and ships that would be searching would not find them.
5. Variety of answers.

Chapter Seven:

1. Timothy jumped into the water so he could kick the raft to shore.
2. Timothy did not seem afraid of sharks because Timothy and Phillip were too close in to shore for sharks to come.
3. Langosta page 60. Variety of descriptions.
4. Phillip felt Timothy knew something that he wasn't sharing with him.
5. Phillip was frightened because he was left alone and helpless on the beach.
6. From Timothy's calculations the island was one mile long and a half mile wide, shaped liked a melon (page 63).
7. The reason it was a mistake to have landed on this island:
   a) no ships will pass close to the island.
   b) they cannot be rescued because of the sharp coral banks on either side.
   c) no one lived on the island.

Chapter Eight:

1. There may not be a search party out looking for the two survivors because all the ships and aircraft were needed to fight the U-boats.
2. Phillip was afraid to be alone because he was afraid something might happen to him.
3. Stew Cat comforted Phillip because he rubbed along his arms and up against his cheek, purring hard (page 69).
4. Things learned about Timothy:
   a) They had their place and we had ours.
   b) Timothy was more than seventy.
   c) It was difficult to understand Timothy because he wasn't always clear.
   d) Timothy couldn't spell.
   e) He was too stubborn to admit he couldn't spell.

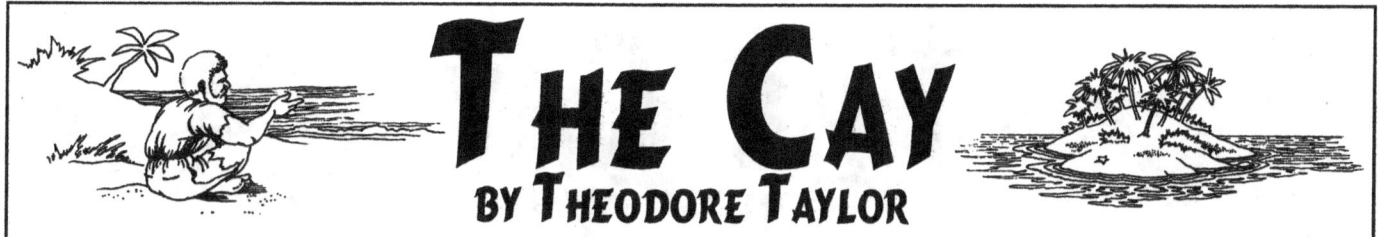

THE CAY
BY THEODORE TAYLOR

Island Rhyme Rescue:
1. fried - dried
2. bonds - fronds
3. calm - palm
4. wire - fire
5. damp - camp
6. found - ground
7. sleeve - weave
8. kind - blind
9. mobster - lobster
10. reach - beach
11. unite - ignite
12. sprawled - crawled
13. moaned - groaned
14. interior - superior
15. tick - stick

True or False:
1. F 2. T 3. T 4. F 5. F 6. F 7. T 8. T 9. F 10. F 11. T 12. T

Chapters Nine and Ten:
1. The rope would be for Phillip to follow if he heard an airplane. He could take a light from the campfire and follow the rope down and touch off the big fire.
2. Timothy expected Phillip to help weave the vines into a rope.
3. Phillip began to change because he started to accept Timothy as a friend.
4. Variety of answers.
5. Two reasons why they were glad to have rain:
   a) to get drinking water.
   b) cools the air.
6. Phillip wanted the rain to continue because it was something he could hear and feel.

Match the Words with the Meanings:
1. catchment	_____	fastened by rope, chain, or thong
2. pompano	12	leaf-like shoot of a palm tree
3. rancid	5	small, round sea animals with sharp spines
4. steel bands	11	indefinitely, uncertainty
5. fronds	8	musical instruments
6. scorpions	4	small islet composed of sand and coral
7. reeve	9	trough to catch and funnel water into a container
8. vaguely	1	kind of fish
9. cay	2	native lobster without claws
10. langosta	10	stale
11. sea urchins	3	poisonous arachnid
12. tethered	6	pass in or through something
	7	

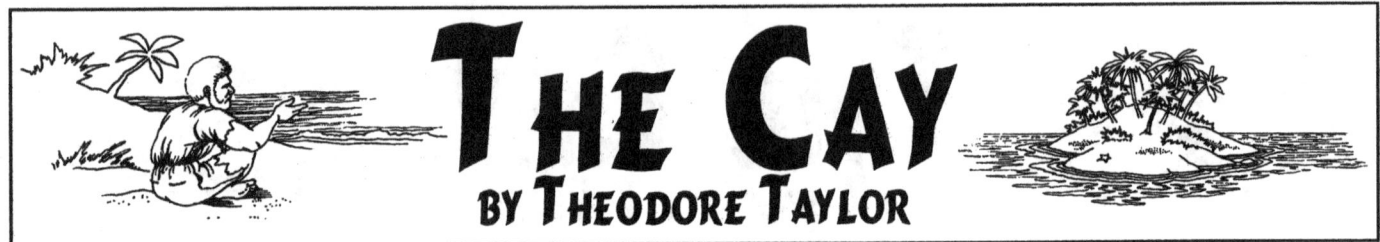

Chapter Eleven:

3. Timothy tried to make Phillip independent because of the possibility of his dying.
4. Timothy thinks Stew Cat is "d'jumbi" because he is superstitious and he thinks he has brought them bad luck.
5. Things Timothy did that made Phillip suspicious of what he had done to Stew Cat are
   a) he was down on the north beach early cutting wood.
   b) the knife was missing.
   c) Stew Cat was missing.
   d) the raft was gone.
6. Phillip could have had an encounter with a skate that has a stinger tail, or with a shark.

Chapter Twelve:

1. Tim was running a fever because he had an attack of malaria.
2. Phillip did for Timothy:
   a) gave him some water.
   b) put a cloth on his forehead.
   c) talked to him.
   d) dragged Timothy out of the water.
   e) covered him with branches of sea grape.
   f) leaned on Phillip for support as he walked back up the hill.
3. Timothy ran into the water because his head was burning with fever.
4. The delirious state was dangerous for both Phillip and Timothy because Timothy was not aware of what he was doing and he could have drowned when he ran in the water.
5. He never really regained his strength means he was in a weakened state since his malaria attack and that could eventually be responsible for his death.

Chapter Thirteen:

1. Phillip kept track of the date because each day he dropped a small pebble into an old can.
2. It was necessary for Phillip to learn how to fish in case Timothy was sick some morning.
3. Nails were made into fish hooks.
4. Sketch.
5. They need to catch a mussel first to use for bait.
6. Fishing feels so special for Phillip because he had fished many times with his father and this was easy. He was learning to do things all over again, by touch and feel.
7. Ways Phillip is maturing as described in this chapter are:
   a) Phillip has learned to fish
   b) Phillip was able to relate to Timothy how the cay developed
   c) Phillip climbed a coconut tree
   d) Phillip now visualizes Timothy as kind and strong, not ugly and black.
8. Phillip wondered if Timothy were the same black man he had been on the raft with because he now appears kind and strong, not ugly like he remembered him.

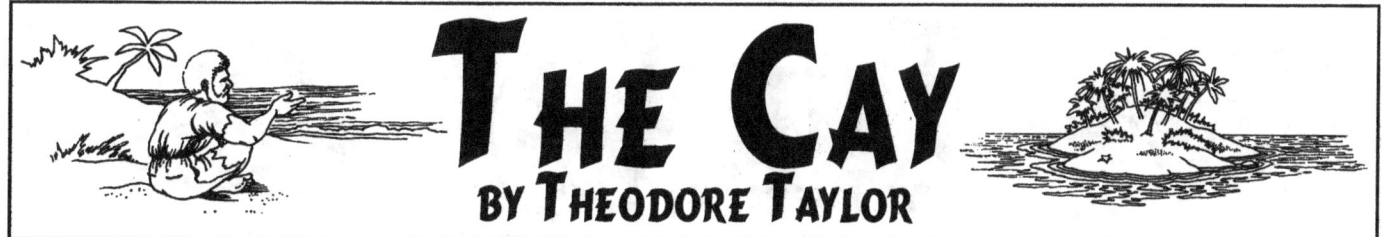

THE CAY
BY THEODORE TAYLOR

Chapter Fourteen:
1. The noise like a rifle was made by the ocean waves.
2. The sound frightened Timothy because it meant a hurricane is building.
3. Signals that proved to Timothy that a hurricane was coming:
   a) the shot like a rifle.
   b) Timothy could smell a change in the air.
   c) there was a breathless silence.
   d) the sea was as smooth as green jelly but the water was cloudy.
   e) there were no birds in sight.
   f) the sky had a yellowish cast to it.
4. The preparations Timothy made as the storm approached:
   a) lashed our water keg high on a palm trunk.
   b) tied the rope around a sturdy tree.
   c) stripped everything usable from the raft.
   d) they had a huge meal because they may not be able to eat for several days.
   e) lashed the tin box high in a tree.

Chapter Fifteen:
1. At sunset the sky was flaming and there were thin veils of high clouds.
2. The sea was beginning to reach for our hilltop climbing the forty feet with raging whitecaps.
3. Phillip was shivering because the rain was icy, he was wet from head to foot and he feared the thought of the sea rolling over them.
4. How strong the wind had become:
   a) the hut had blown away
   b) there was no sound now except the roar of the storm
   c) sea grape was being torn up by the roots.
5. Timothy saved them by tying them to a palm tree.
6. There was a calm time for about 20 or 30 minutes because it was the eye of the hurricane which is the centre of the storm.
7. Tim's back bled because the wind drove the rain and tiny grains of sand so strongly against his back.
8. Stew Cat survived the hurricane in a palm tree. Variety of answers.
9. At the end of the chapter Timothy died.
10. Words to describe Timothy. Variety of answers.
11. The small happy event that comforted Phillip was Stew Cat returned safely.

Chapter Sixteen:
1. Littered with debris means scattered with all kinds of pieces of palm branches, sticks, driftwood, shells, or coral; things are very disorganized.
2. He meant if Phillip could have seen everything he would have been very frightened. His blindness protected him.
3. Timothy trained Phillip carefully so he would be able to survive if something happened to him.
4. The Cay was recovering. Variety of answers.
5. Things Phillip found as he explored the island were large cans, old broom, small wooden crate, piece of canvas, shells, pieces of cork, bodies of dead birds, chunks of sponge.
6. Phillip was like the birds because they were fighting for survival just as he was.

Chapter Seventeen:
1. The quote was humorous because Stew Cat couldn't save Phillip.
2. Phillip decided to stop eating coconuts because there were only a few left on the cay.
3. Phillip couldn't obtain scallops because they were off the north beach and there was the danger of sharks there.
4. Phillip decided to go in the "fishing hole" because he wanted to catch a langosta clinging to coral.
5. Phillip was safe in the fishing hole from:
   sharks - too large to swim through the narrow sea entrance to the fishing hole
   barracuda - could swim into the fishing hole but they were not usually dangerous
   octopus - If there was one it would be small. The big ones preferred deep water.

Chapter Eighteen:
1. Phillip was able to achieve the dark smoke to attract the airplane by green palm fronds or sea grape.
2. Phillip used to explain the sounds:
   birds - different cries
   breeze - fluttered the small leaves
   airplane - drone of the motor
   signal fire - crackle of flames, roaring
3. Phillip's rescue seemed hopeless because no one or no thing saw his signal fire so no one knew he was a survivor.
4. Variety of answers.

THE CAY
BY THEODORE TAYLOR

Chapter Nineteen:
1. He made that observation because of the way Phillip approached him and the fact he was naked and it didn't bother him.
2. The people Phillip spoke to would have trouble understanding what happened on the cay because of how long they survived on such a small cay and the primitive conditions they lived under.
3. Variety of answers.

Sequence of Events:
5, 2, 8, 11, 3, 10, 9, 1, 6, 12, 4, 7

Word Search:

```
P O R T M O R A Y E E L P V
N R S N O I P R O C S A C E
F T R E N C H W L A R O Q E
R A N C I D U E L T O N M R
O B E T S R A L U C O N I B
N O D E P R O T B H D Y E O
D U A L W O N A P M O P B O
S I G N A L F I R E O T O T
G M N K S T E R N N V S N S
S A U B A L L A S T D H Y G
T R B D K I Y L E E W A R D
O O P L G E N A C I R R U H
B O W S H E Y M C T P K I N
S N I H C R U A E S T A C K
```

Mystery Words:
DEVIL'S MOUTH

The Winning Effort:
1. shout, shouted, shouting
2. flap, flapped, flapping
3. fit, fitted, fitting
4. extend, extended, extending
5. murmur, murmured, murmuring
6. submerge, submerged, submerging
7. drop, dropped, dropping
8. protest, protested, protesting
9. smolder, smoldered, smoldering
10. awaken, awakened, awakening
11. discuss, discussed, discussing
12. explode, exploded, exploding
13. connive, connived, conniving
14. plan, planned, planning
15. separate, separated, separating
16. convince, convinced, convincing
17. frighten, frightened, frightening
18. echo, echoed, echoing
19. salvage, salvaged, salvaging
20. fascinate, fascinated, fascinating

Math to the Rescue - Secret Message:
THEY'RE BOTH LOOKING FOR A SALE (SAIL)

THE CAY
BY THEODORE TAYLOR

www.ingramcontent.com/pod-product-compliance
Lightning Source LLC
Chambersburg PA
CBHW081325020726

47506CB00005B/1181